The Search for the
Snow Monkey

Written by AnnMarie Anderson

Illustrated by Carrie English

Sam & Sofia's Scooter Stories

First paperback edition printed in 2019 by Little Passports, Inc.
Copyright © 2019 Little Passports
All rights reserved
Book design by Carly Queen
Manufactured in China
10 9 8

Little Passports, Inc.
27 Maiden Lane, Suite 400, San Francisco, CA 94108
www.littlepassports.com
ISBN: 978-1-953148-01-8

Contents

1 A Model Idea 1
2 Welcome to Japan 13
3 Origami Surprise 22
4 A Snowy Start 34
5 Cooking Class 43
6 Sofia's Big Save 53
7 Monkey Mischief 65
8 Sam's Big Save 75
9 Sayonara, Japan! 81
10 Painting Perfection 88
11 Home Again 97

1
A Model Idea

Sam scaled the ladder of branches sprouting from the giant oak tree in his front yard. It was the largest tree on Compass Court and Sam's favorite climbing spot. He settled himself against the trunk and pointed the zoom lens of his camera at Compass Community Center.

Click-click! Click-click!

Sam snapped a few photos of his nearly finished mural on the side of the building. He saw the green-gray body of the crocodile from Africa, then zoomed in to look at its crooked teeth—**click-click!** He moved over to the curved tail of the Australian kangaroo—**click-click!**—the white feathers of the American bald eagle—**click-click!**—and the spotted face of the panda from China—**click-click!**

Some animals needed a touch-up here or there, but from his perch in the tree, Sam thought they all looked pretty good. There was one problem, though.

Sam moved his camera over to the Japanese macaque

and sighed. Zooming in, he could see the snow monkey's fuzzy body, its short, stubby tail, and its completely wrong, completely unfinished face. Sam and his best friend Sofia had been painting all week, and he still couldn't get the macaque's face quite right.

Sam thought looking at the macaque from a monkey's-eye view would give him some inspiration, but he still felt stumped. What was he going to do? The mural was called *Animals Around the World*. It wasn't called *Animals Around the World, Except for Japan Because the Monkey Was Too Hard*. And he didn't have much time to figure it out, either. The mural was going to be unveiled tonight in front of the whole neighborhood!

"Sam?" came a voice from the foot of the tree. "Are you up there?"

"Yup! Coming down," Sam said, jumping to the ground to meet his aunt.

Aunt Charlie was a scientist and an inventor. She had just stepped out of her garage-turned-lab wearing a white coat covered in paint splatters.

"Do you think this might help?" she asked, holding up a jar of rust-colored paint. "I just mixed it up. You can't paint a perfect macaque face without the perfect color."

And it really did look perfect.

"Thanks, Aunt Charlie," Sam said. "I'm gonna try it right now!"

Sam put the jar of paint in his messenger bag and headed off toward the mural.

"Good luck!" Aunt Charlie called, turning back to her lab.

As he walked across Compass Court toward the community center, Sam imagined painting the color on the wall with a fine brush to get all the small details of the macaque's face. He'd need something precise. Something with a very small tip. Something exactly like the brush suddenly thrust in front of his face!

Sam stopped and turned. His best friend Sofia was holding the brush. Her hair was pulled back with a bright blue headband that matched her overalls. "I borrowed some supplies from my dad," she said enthusiastically.

Sofia's dad was an artist. His studio was full of materials. Sofia pulled more paintbrushes from

one of her many pockets. "I have others, too."

"This one's perfect," Sam said. "You read my mind. I need the fine tip for the snow monkey's face. Aunt Charlie even mixed us a custom paint color!"

The two friends hurried to the mural. Sam pulled the jar of reddish-brown paint from his bag while Sofia immediately got to work. She added detail to the bamboo around the panda, finished outlining the feathers of the macaw, and painted more grass around the feet of the elephant.

Meanwhile, Sam just stood there. He stood and stared at the space where the monkey's face should be. By the time Sofia moved on to the leaves around the toucan, she knew something was up.

"What's wrong?" she asked him.

Sam just shook his head. He had the perfect paint and the perfect brush, but finishing this

animal seemed impossible.

"I'm not sure," he said. "The snow monkey has such an expressive face. And the rest of the mural is almost done. I just want it to be perfect for the unveiling."

"I know what you mean," Sofia said, tapping her chin with a paintbrush. "It needs to look alive. You could really use a monkey model."

Sam laughed at the thought of a monkey posing for him as he painted.

"Wait, that's it," Sam said slowly. "A live model!"

Sofia tapped her paintbrush against her chin again, dotting her face with green paint. "But the zoo doesn't have snow monkeys, remember?"

Sam's eyes twinkled with excitement.

"Who said anything about the zoo?" he asked, raising an eyebrow.

He and Sofia exchanged a look. Then they both broke into huge grins.

"*Vamos!*" Sofia said, and the pair hurried back to Sam's house. They both knew their ticket to finding a live snow monkey model was in Aunt Charlie's lab.

Sam and Sofia burst into the garage. Sam breathed a sigh of relief when he saw that Aunt Charlie wasn't inside. She had probably gone to help Sofia's mom get ready for tonight's unveiling.

Sam and Sofia headed to a corner of the lab where a big blue tarp was draped over a large object. Sam pulled off the tarp to reveal a shiny candy-apple-red scooter.

This was no ordinary electric scooter. Aunt Charlie had programmed the vehicle to travel anywhere in the world in an instant. Sam wasn't sure if Aunt Charlie knew he and Sofia had once borrowed it to travel to Brazil, but he knew his aunt loved adventures. And she trusted him. Since visiting Brazil, Sam thought of the world as a wonderland waiting to be explored, and he knew Aunt Charlie believed that, too.

Sofia leaned over and tapped the shiny touch screen mounted on the handlebars. The screen lit up like an invitation.

"Ready?" Sam asked Sofia as he climbed onto the scooter.

She hopped on behind him.

"Ready!" she replied.

As soon as they were seated, a rotating globe appeared on the screen, followed by familiar yellow letters.

Sam quickly typed a reply:

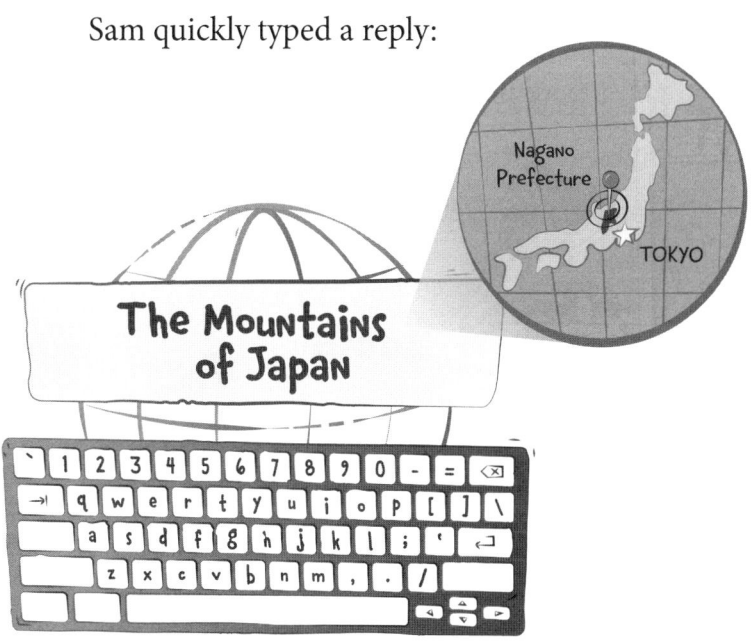

The globe expanded, zooming in on the country of Japan. A blinking dot hovered over Nagano Prefecture, north of Tokyo. A large green button flashed on the screen.

"Hold on tight," Sam said. "Here we go!"

He took a deep breath and pressed the green button. The glittering glow of the touch screen brightened, the scooter's headlamps and taillights shined in great beams, and a shimmering orb of light swirled around the scooter. Soon it was so bright Sam had to close his eyes.

The scooter rumbled beneath them.

Whiz ... Zoom ... Foop!

2
Welcome to Japan

When Sam opened his eyes, he and Sofia were no longer in Aunt Charlie's lab. Instead, the scooter sat on a snow-covered road stretching over a small river. Red railings lined a bridge leading into a tiny town. Near the bridge, a large sign welcomed visitors. At least Sam thought it did—the words were written in Japanese!

"Wow," Sam said in awe, blinking at the scooter's screen again. "I don't think I'll ever get over how cool that is."

"Aunt Charlie's a genius," Sofia agreed, looking around her in wonder. "It's snowing! I wonder how close we are to the snow monkeys."

The last time Sam and Sofia hopped on Aunt Charlie's scooter, they had ended up in Sofia's father's hometown of São Paulo, Brazil.

"I don't know," Sam said. "I told the scooter to take us to the mountains, but I'm not sure how we'll find the monkeys."

"Too bad we can't read that sign," Sofia said, as she and Sam hopped off the scooter.

Ahead of them, small two-story buildings lined a narrow street. Red paper lanterns hung from the pointed wooden eaves, giving the village a festive look. Dark wooden signs painted with Japanese writing framed many of the doorways.

Sofia rubbed her arms and looked at the white-capped mountains across the river.

"Brrr," she said. "We should have brought warmer clothes."

"Who says we didn't?" Sam said with a smile. Sofia gave him a curious look.

Sam popped open a secret compartment beneath the scooter's seat and pulled out his bulging messenger bag. "After our trip to Brazil, I packed some stuff we might need for other trips." He rummaged through the bag. "Snacks, water, a first aid kit, drawing supplies, of course . . ."

"Of course," Sofia agreed.

"And . . . clothes!"

He handed Sofia a warm vest and put on one he'd packed for himself. Finally, he tucked a sketchpad and pencils in the messenger bag's front pocket, slung it over his shoulder, and snapped the scooter's compartment shut.

"Good thinking, Sam," said Sofia. "I was about to freeze."

"You know me," Sam said, lifting his camera. "I like to be prepared. Say cheese!"

Sofia zipped up her vest. "Cheesecake!"

Click-click!

"Should we explore a little?" Sofia asked.

They parked the scooter next to a row of bicycles on the side of the road and headed into town. They walked down the narrow streets, taking in their surroundings. Sam photographed the snow-covered roofs of the cozy-looking buildings and the sparkling icicles hanging from the eaves. Despite the cold, the village felt warm and welcoming. Wooden doors slid open and closed as people came and went. People nodded at them and smiled as they passed.

"I wish we knew where to look for the monkeys," Sofia said.

Sam couldn't wait to find a real live Japanese macaque. He knew the monkeys lived in the snowy mountains of Japan, but he wasn't sure how to find them. Then he noticed a staircase along the side of the street. Maybe he and Sofia

could get a bird's-eye view of the town, just like when he'd climbed the tree back home on Compass Court.

"Let's try those steps," Sam suggested. "Maybe we'll get a better view up there."

"Great idea," Sofia agreed.

They climbed the steep, narrow steps, being careful not to slip on patches of ice. When they got to the top, they found themselves in a plaza overlooking a small valley. Below them, Sam and Sofia could see the snow-blanketed rooftops of the village surrounded by hills. To Sam's right, some trails led into a grove of trees.

"You think any macaques live over there?" Sam asked, pointing to the grove.

"Maybe," Sofia said. "It looks pretty empty, though."

Sam looked through the zoom lens of his camera, hoping to catch a glimpse of something small and furry in the trees. He didn't see anything—he heard something instead! A loud shout echoed up from the streets below, followed by a crash.

"What was that?" Sam asked. He and Sofia rushed to the edge of the plaza, leaning far over the railing.

"I can't see anything," Sofia said.

It sounded like someone—or something—was making its way through the streets below, slamming into things at every turn. A series of yelps and shouts moved quickly from one side of the village to the other. After a few more seconds, the commotion was right below them!

"There's only one way to find out what's going on," Sam said.

"Follow that noise!" Sofia said.

Sam and Sofia hurried down the steps after the commotion. Sam moved quickly—too quickly! His sneakers slipped down the icy steps, and when he reached the bottom, he slid wildly across a huge patch of ice. Sofia skidded along right behind him, the two twirling through the snow. Sofia yelped. Sam reached out to steady himself as something darted in front of them. They were sliding right toward a tree, and they were about to crash!

3
Origami Surprise

At the last moment, Sam reached out and grabbed a low-hanging branch. He and Sofia slammed to a stop, barely missing the tree's trunk as a figure rushed past them. Snow sprinkled down from the branches above as the two caught their breath.

"That was close," Sofia said.

Just ahead, a girl dashed off as if she was running after—or away from—something. Had she been the one crashing through the village?

Sam quickly glanced at Sofia. From the look on her face, he could tell she was wondering the same thing. The girl made a sharp left and headed down an alley. Sam shook the snow from his hair and turned to follow her, with Sofia close behind. The cold air stung his cheeks and burned his lungs as he ran. He tried to keep up, but the girl was fast. She made another sharp turn, this time down a narrow passageway to the right. Sam slowed to steady himself on another patch of ice, and when he looked up, the girl was gone. He stopped abruptly and Sofia bumped into him again, both of them sliding in the snow.

"Good thing these vests are puffy," she said, panting.

"I should've packed better shoes," Sam said.

Sofia spun around, still breathing heavily. "Where did she go?"

Sam bent over, resting his hands on his knees.

"I—" He gasped for air. "I don't know."

Sofia wiped snow from her legs.

"Maybe she went inside one of these houses," she said. "She probably lives around here."

Another shout echoed through the streets. Sam and Sofia exchanged a glance.

"*Vamos!*" Sofia said. She sprinted down the street toward the voice, and Sam followed close behind. A few seconds later, they skidded to a stop.

"I think that's her," Sofia said.

She pointed toward the building in front of them. Through a crack in the sliding door, they saw a girl about their age inside.

"Wow..." Sam's mouth dropped open as he peered through the door's opening.

"How cool!"

Inside, the walls were lined with shelves of brightly colored origami creations. Sam had folded simple origami pieces in an art class at Compass Community Center back home, but nothing as detailed as this! He marveled at the displays. There were birds, dogs, insects, cranes, boats, and dragons, and every single creation was made entirely from intricately folded paper.

On one wall stood a bookshelf with step-by-step instruction books. A rack of patterned paper sat opposite the bookshelf.

The main display was a wooden table standing in the center of the room. At least, it used to be standing. It was now tipped on its side, and origami was scattered all over the floor. Sam and Sofia watched the girl hurry back and forth inside the shop, picking up the fallen origami.

"*Gomen nasai,*" the girl said to an older woman standing behind a long counter. The woman stepped into the center of the store and turned the wooden table right-side up.

"Hello . . ." Sam said, waving

hesitantly from the doorway. "Do you need some help?"

"Oh!" the girl said, startled. "*Hai*. Yes, thank you."

Sam and Sofia stepped inside, collected some paper animals, and placed them gently on the table.

"I'm Sam," Sam said to the girl. "And this is my friend Sofia."

Sofia smiled. "Nice to meet you."

"I'm Hana," the girl said. "Thank you for your help."

"Sure," Sam said. "It's no trouble."

Hana smiled at them, but she seemed sad.

"We saw you running through the village," Sofia said. "Is everything okay?"

"I feel terrible," Hana said, tears in her eyes. "A naughty *saru* stole one of my mother's *kokeshi* dolls. She has a whole collection. She loves those dolls! I was chasing the *saru* and it ran in here and made this mess. And it got away with my mother's doll!"

"A *saru*?" Sam asked.

"A monkey," Hana explained. "Those macaques are always causing trouble."

"You were chasing a snow monkey?" Sam gasped, his eyes lighting up.

Sofia jabbed her elbow into Sam's side.

"*Oof!*" Sam cleared his throat. "I mean, I'm sorry about your mother's doll."

The shopkeeper patted Hana gently on the arm.

"Your mother will understand, Hana-chan," she said. "It wasn't your fault."

Hana hung her head.

"That's just it," she said. "It *was* my fault! It was my job to keep the monkeys out of the inn this morning. But I got distracted. My mother loves that doll."

"Excuse me, but what's a *kokeshi* doll?"

Sofia asked, curious.

Hana smiled. "It's a traditional wooden doll. *Kokeshi* come from Tōhoku, an area north of here, where my mother was born."

"The dolls are shaped simply, with just a head and body," the shopkeeper explained. "Many are carved or painted with pretty designs. Your mother's collection is beautiful," she added to Hana. "I've seen the display at your family's *ryokan*."

"*Ryokan*?" Sam repeated.

"A traditional Japanese inn," Hana said. "My family has owned the inn for years."

"Maybe the doll isn't lost forever," Sam said. "Can't we try to get it back?"

The shopkeeper's gentle laugh rang through the shop.

"That monkey is long gone, like a rabbit down a hole," she said. "It's probably up in the mountains by now."

Hana nodded. "I'm sorry again about the origami display."

"There's no reason to worry," the woman said. She lifted an origami crane from the floor and smoothed its wings. "It's only paper."

But Sam wasn't willing to give up on the doll—or the monkey—so fast.

"If the monkey lives in the mountains, we can follow it," he said eagerly. "What if we help you find the monkey and the doll before your mom finds out it's missing?"

"Really?" Hana asked. "Do you think we could?"

Sam nodded. "We were actually hoping to see some Japanese macaques," he said. "It's the reason we came to Japan. We'd be happy to help find the doll along the way."

"I don't know," Hana said. "It would be awfully hard to find the monkey again. I should probably just go home and tell my mother what happened to her *kokeshi* doll."

"Please," Sofia said. "Let's just try. I know we can help."

"And you're our best shot at finding the monkeys we came all this way to see," Sam added.

Hana looked at Sam and Sofia thoughtfully. Would Hana agree to their offer, or would their search for the snow monkey be over before it even started?

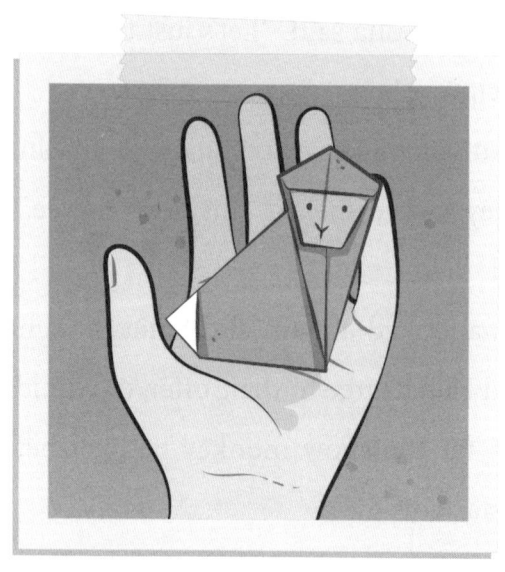

4
A Snowy Start

After a moment, Hana smiled.

"Okay," she agreed. "We can try."

"Great!" Sam said, probably a little too loudly.

"We'll find the doll together," Sofia added.

"Thank you for offering to help," said Hana.

"That's very kind."

The shopkeeper smiled warmly at the three of them.

"If you want to find the snow monkeys and the doll, follow the trail at the edge of town, just past Nagano Café," she said. "It leads to the monkeys' hot spring in the mountains."

Before Sam, Sofia, and Hana turned to leave, the shopkeeper placed a tiny gray and white paper monkey in the palm of Sam's hand.

"For you," she said. "Our macaques can be very cute when they aren't being a nuisance."

"Wow," he said softly. Sam carefully turned the monkey over in his hands. It was amazing to think this detailed little snow monkey had once been a simple, flat square of paper.

Sam turned to Hana. "How do I say 'thank you' in Japanese?"

"*Arigatō gozaimasu*," Hana said, adding a slight bow.

Sam turned to the shopkeeper and bowed politely. "*Arigatō gozaimasu,*" he repeated.

The woman smiled. "Good luck finding that monkey. And be careful! It's starting to snow again. The path isn't always clear, and you don't want to get lost in the cold!"

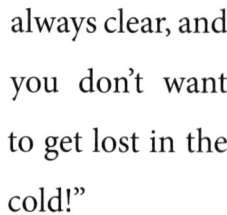

Sam and Sofia followed Hana out of the origami shop and into the cold. Snowflakes danced through the air as Hana motioned for Sam and Sofia to follow her down the street. Up ahead, Sam could see the snow-covered hills rising above the village. As they walked, they passed a group of women wearing cotton robes and wooden sandals, each carrying a small towel.

"They're going for a bath," Hana said. She pointed to a small wooden building ahead of them.

"A bath?" Sam asked in surprise. "When it's snowing outside?"

Hana laughed. "Many people come here to visit our inns and bathhouses, especially in the winter," she explained. "People also come to see the monkeys. They have their own hot spring bath in the mountains."

"Really?" Sofia asked, giggling.

Hana nodded. "It's true."

"People don't take baths at home?" Sam asked as he snapped a shot of the building surrounded by falling snow and wisps of steam.

Click-click!

"They do," Hana explained. "But here in Shibu Onsen, we have many natural hot springs,

or *onsen*. These waters flow to nine different bathhouses. The waters are special because they contain minerals that have healing powers. People come here to soak in the hot springs as a way to relax and feel healthy."

"What are they wearing?" Sam asked. He had never seen wooden sandals before.

"The shoes are called *geta*," Hana replied. "And those kimonos are called *yukata*. Bathers wear them when they walk from one bathhouse to the next."

"And the monkeys have their own *onsen* in the mountains?" Sofia asked.

"They do," Hana said. "But they don't wear *yukata* or *geta*!"

Sam, Sofia, and Hana laughed together at the thought of a macaque in wooden shoes. Sam was glad to see his new friend smiling after she'd been so sad in the origami shop. The three friends continued to chat and tell jokes as they made their way across town.

Before long, they came to a small bridge stretching over the town's river. The bridge led to a system of trails winding into the woods. Hana led Sam and Sofia across the bridge, but she paused at the trailhead. The snow was falling more heavily now, and it was getting hard to see.

"Hmmm," Hana said. "I'm not sure which way to go."

Sam and Sofia looked around the trailhead for clues.

"The shop owner was right," Sam said. "The path isn't very clear." He squinted as he looked around for a sign.

"Are the trails marked?" Sofia asked.

"I thought they were," Hana said, confused. "But it's been a while since I've walked through these trees. And there's so much fresh snow, I can't see any footsteps on any of the trails! What are we going to do?"

The snow was so thick Sam could barely see

the trees around them. But then he noticed a yellow light glowing just ahead, not far from the trailhead. It glittered in the falling snow like an invitation.

5
Cooking Class

"**L**ook!" Sam said to Hana, pointing toward the light. "Any idea what that is?"

"Oh!" Hana replied. "That's Nagano Café. I'm sure someone there will know the way to the monkeys."

The three friends hurried through the snow and ducked inside the café. The small restaurant was bustling with people. A large group of tourists had just arrived, and they were busy taking their seats. A tall man scurried around the restaurant, serving tea.

"That's Mr. Ogawa," Hana said. "He's been serving food here for years."

Hana tried to get Mr. Ogawa's attention, but he was too busy to notice. He walked right past her and turned to a tour guide, who was placing an order.

"A dozen of your famous *onsen-tamago*, please," the tour guide said. "It's too snowy to hike right now, so we figured we'd stop for a snack!"

Mr. Ogawa took his hat off and patted the sweat from his brow. Then he ducked into the nearby kitchen and spoke urgently with the chef. Sam, Sofia, and Hana watched and waited.

"What's going on?" Sam whispered to Hana.

"The chef ran out of his specialty dish," Hana explained. "Eggs soft-boiled in one of the town's hot springs." She leaned closer to the kitchen to hear the rest of the conversation. "They're short-staffed today, so the chef can't fill the tour guide's order."

Mr. Ogawa returned to the counter, barely glancing at Sam, Sofia, and Hana as he dished mounds of noodles into bowls.

Mr. Ogawa looked up. "Can I help you?" he asked them at last.

"We need directions, please," Sofia said.

"We're looking for the snow monkeys that live nearby," Hana added.

"Can you tell us which path to take through the trees?" Sofia asked.

"I'm so sorry," Mr. Ogawa said, "but I don't think I have time right now. Do you mind waiting?"

"I see you're busy," Hana replied, nodding

slowly. She looked at Sam and Sofia, and her eyes lit up. "Maybe we can help you, though!"

Mr. Ogawa paused, noodles dangling above a bowl. He glanced at Hana.

"I'm listening," he said.

"I know how to make *onsen-tamago* in the hot spring," Hana said. "If my friends and I cook the eggs for you, will you point us toward the snow monkeys?"

"We can cook the eggs on the stove," Mr. Ogawa said, "but these people have come all the way to Nagano Café for our famous *onsen-tamago*, and that's what I want to give them." He looked at the three friends skeptically. "The hot spring where we cook the eggs is on the other side of town. Are you sure you're up to the task?"

Hana nodded firmly. "We can do it."

He ladled some dipping sauce into more bowls and placed them next to the noodles. Sam was certain he was going to shoo them away, but

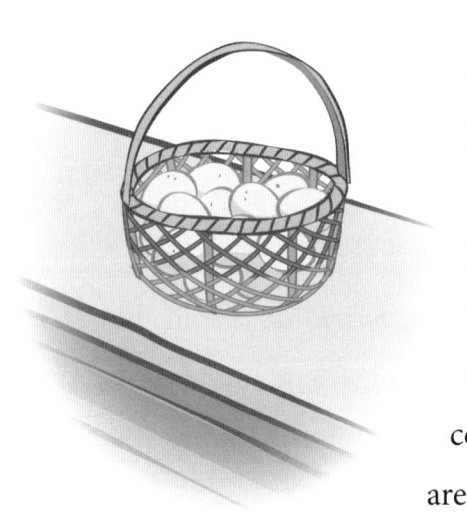

after a moment, Mr. Ogawa straightened his hat and chuckled.

"What an offer!" he said. "How can I say no?" He pointed to a basket on the counter. "Those eggs are nice and fresh. Hurry to the hot spring, cook them up, and bring them back. I'll let this group know we'll have our special *onsen-tamago* for them after all!"

"Great!" Hana said. Then she turned to Sam and Sofia. "Ready for another adventure?"

"Always," Sam replied eagerly.

"Let's do it," Sofia agreed. "*Vamos!*"

Hana grabbed the basket, and the three friends headed back outside. The snow was still falling, but it was a bit lighter now. Hana walked quickly, and Sam and Sofia dashed after her to keep up, zipping their vests tight as they went.

"How far is it?" Sofia asked.

"Not too far," Hana replied. "The village isn't very big."

"How do you cook an egg in a hot spring?" Sam asked. His sneakers crunched in the fresh snow as he hurried along.

"You place the eggs in the hot water for a few minutes," Hana explained. "The egg yolk cooks before the white, so the egg stays soft and silky. Then you remove the shell and eat the egg with rice or broth. Yum!"

"That sounds delicious," Sam agreed. "And warm." He shivered and put his hands in his pockets. The snow was still falling around them, and Sam stomped his feet to keep them warm as he walked. In the distance, he saw wisps of

steam rising between some pine trees.

"Is that the hot spring?" he asked Hana, squinting through the snow.

"Yes, that's it," Hana said. She stopped near three steamy pools of water. Hana walked a few steps to the largest pool, Sam and Sofia following.

"This spring water is too hot to bathe in," she said. "But people come here to cook eggs and vegetables. The eggs need to cook for ten minutes in water this hot."

Sam held up his watch.

"I can time it," he offered.

"Great!" Hana replied. She gently lowered the basket of eggs into the hot water as Sam clicked the button on his watch. The trio waited as the timer counted down and the eggs cooked. It seemed to take forever! Sam watched with excitement as the timer finally clicked down to zero.

"Five, four, three, two, DONE!" he cried.

Hana pulled the basket upward, but something was wrong. "Oh!" she cried, tugging at the basket.

"What is it?" Sam asked.

"The basket," Hana said. "It's stuck!"

6
Sofia's Big Save

"Let me take a look," Sofia said.

"Quick, Sofia. We're almost out of time!" Sam said.

Sofia leaned over the steamy pool to examine the basket. "The handle's caught on a rock," she said, "and it's starting to tear! If I could just reach in there . . ."

"No, don't!" Hana cried. "You'll burn your hand."

Sofia tapped her chin thoughtfully. Then she began pulling things out of her pockets. "*Hmm*. I'm sure I have something useful in here."

First came a large button, then a few safety pins.

"Hurry," Hana urged her. "If we don't get the eggs out soon, they'll overcook!"

"The basket's going to break," Sofia said. "We'll need something new."

Sofia jumped into action. She reached over to Sam's vest, grabbed the string laced through the front of the hood, and yanked.

"Hey!" Sam said.

The string slipped completely from the hood. Sofia reached back and grabbed her own hood, unsnapping it from her vest. She quickly tied Sam's loose string to the one on her hood.

"We're running out of time," Hana said, bouncing on her feet.

"Almost done." Sofia looped the ends of the strings through the holes in the large button and secured them with a safety pin. The detached hood now looked like a basket, with the two connected cords as the handle.

Sofia quickly lowered the hood into the water and, tipping the basket, she nudged the eggs inside the fabric.

"There!" Sofia said, pulling the hood up out of the water. The eggs were safely inside.

"Wow," Hana said. "That was really clever."

"That's Sofia," Sam said proudly. "She can make something out of anything."

"You really saved the day," Hana said. "Now we'd better get back quickly. I hope we still have a chance of finding that monkey—and my mother's doll!"

The trio hurried back through the snowy

streets as quickly as they could. In no time, Sam saw the bright, glowing lights of the café appear through the falling snow. Hana pushed open the door and a bell hanging over the doorway jangled cheerily. Mr. Ogawa smiled from behind the counter as Hana, Sam, and Sofia stepped into the warm café.

"Perfect timing!" he said, hurrying over to grab the eggs. "Can you three help me for one more minute? I promise I'll show you where you want to go afterward."

The three friends looked at each other.

"Okay," Sam said. "What do you need?"

"I need someone to serve tea. Just refill cups," he explained, waving his hat toward the other guests. "I'll crack an egg into each bowl. One of you can pour the *soy-dashi* broth over the eggs while the other sprinkles scallions on top."

"Got it," Sam said, nodding.

"I'm on tea," Sofia said. "I love tea time." She

picked up the teapot and headed over to the table of guests.

"I'll take care of the broth," Hana said.

"Great," Sam said. "I'll do the scallions, then."

Hana picked up a ladle and poured broth over each egg as Mr. Ogawa handed her the bowls. Sam sprinkled the eggs with plenty of chopped scallions. Finally, Sam placed the finished bowls on a large tray.

When Sofia returned with the empty teapot, the bowls of *onsen-tamago* were ready.

"Wonderful!" Mr. Ogawa said. Then he picked up the tray and whirled around to deliver the dishes to the waiting customers.

"I hope he really knows the way to the snow monkeys," Sam said. He felt a bit worried as he, Sofia, and Hana waited for Mr. Ogawa to return, but it didn't take long. A moment later, Mr. Ogawa was back.

"Thank you for your help," Mr. Ogawa said. "I couldn't have done everything so quickly without you three. Now, remind me," he said, wiping his hands on his apron. "Where are you going?"

"We're headed to see the snow monkeys," Hana said.

"What an idea," Mr. Ogawa said. "Very poor customers, snow monkeys. They're always making a mess. You sure you want to find them?"

"Very sure," Sam said.

"Okay, then," Mr. Ogawa said. "Follow me." He led the three to the door and stepped outside.

"The monkeys live near the mountain hot spring," he said, pointing through the fallen snow. "Cross the wooden bridge there and take the path to the right. You'll walk for a while before you get to some cliffs. There, you'll find a second bridge, which will lead you to the hot spring where the monkeys like to play. But first," he said, spinning around with a grin, "have some *onsen-tamago*!"

He shuffled them back into the café and sat them in chairs right at the counter. Then he

placed a bowl in front of each of them.

"*Itadakimasu*," Hana said.

Mr. Ogawa smiled in reply.

"I know we have to get going, but this looks so good," Sam said, picking up his spoon. "I didn't realize I was so hungry."

"A quick bite," Hana said.

"It's the polite thing to do," Sofia agreed, already stuffing a napkin in her shirt.

Sam used his spoon to cut into the egg. The bright yellow yolk was thick and smooth, like custard. Sam scooped up a bit with some broth and scallions and took a bite. **Sluuurrp.** "This is one of the best eggs I've ever tasted."

"I love *onsen-tamago*," Hana agreed.

Sofia finished her egg in a few bites. "That was deee-lish!" she said wiping her mouth.

Sam and Hana laughed.

"What do you say at the end of a meal in Japan?" Sam asked Hana.

"*Gochisosama*," Hana said. "It means 'thank you for the meal.'"

"*Gochisosama,*" Sam and Sofia said together.

Then the three friends got up and turned to head to the mountain trail.

"The sun is going to set soon," Hana pointed out. "We'll have to walk fast to get there and back before dark."

Sam and Sofia quickly zipped their vests and followed Hana to the door.

"Wait!" Mr. Ogawa cried, hurrying over. "Take these Nagano apples for a snack. They're grown right here in town! And thank you again for your help."

Sam smiled at Mr. Ogawa, bowed gratefully, and said, "*Arigatō gozaimasu.*"

Mr. Ogawa bowed in return before swiveling around to pour more tea for his guests. Sam slipped the apples into his bag and followed Sofia and Hana into the snowy afternoon.

Hana led the way over the bridge and up the path to the right. The snow had picked up again, swirling in flurries, with flakes floating to the ground all around them. At first, the three friends walked quickly through the trees. But as they went on, the path grew steeper and narrower, and their pace slowed.

"Phew," Sofia said. "I'm glad we had a warm meal. Searching for snow monkeys is hard work."

Sam paused to catch his breath. "But the faster we walk," he said, "the warmer we are!"

Sam looked up into the trees that stood straight and tall all around them, their branches dusted with fresh snow. Suddenly, there was a flash of gray up ahead.

"Did you see what I just saw?!" Sam cried.

"There!" Sofia said.

"I see it!" said Hana.

7
Monkey Mischief

Sam picked up the pace and hurried up the snowy path. Sofia and Hana scurried after him.

"There it is again!" Sofia said. Sam glanced up just in time to see a monkey disappear into the trees. He pulled out his camera. He wanted to be ready once he got close enough for a good shot.

"Hurry," Hana said. "I'll bet that one will lead us right to the monkeys' *onsen*!"

Sam imagined seeing the macaque in person and getting the perfect photo to help him finish his mural back home. With a burst of energy, he sprinted ahead of Sofia and Hana, his camera bouncing against his chest.

"Come on, slowpokes!" he called back.

He kept catching glimpses of the monkey through the trees. Or, wait a minute . . .

"There are two of them!" Sam cried. "We must be getting close!"

Sam watched as the monkeys paused from time to time, peeking back at him through the patches of snow, almost as if they were waiting for him to catch up.

"I think they're playing!" Sofia said.

Click-click!

Sam snapped a quick photo before the monkeys sprang forward, as if daring him to follow.

"You're right!" Sam said. The three friends ran after the pair of monkeys, trying hard not to lose sight of them.

A moment later, the trees opened up to a wooden bridge over a flowing river.

"We must be almost there," Hana said. "The monkeys' *onsen* is just across the second bridge, remember?" She lowered her voice to a whisper. "Let's go quietly so we don't scare them off."

Steam from the hot water rose up in curls as Sam, Sofia, and Hana crossed the bridge.

On the other side, Sam stopped in his tracks. "Wow," he breathed, amazed.

Just beyond the bridge was a pool of water. The hot spring was surrounded by rocks. There

were monkeys everywhere! Some bathed in the water, while others sat on the rocks grooming one another. A few monkeys hopped between the rocks and the trees and the edge of the pool.

Click-click! Click-click!

Sam walked around, trying to snap images of the monkeys' faces from every angle. Seeing them face-to-face was unbelievable. He could see the expressive lines around their mouths, the soft texture of their fur, and the mischievous sparkle in their eyes, as if they were in the middle of thinking up fun pranks. If the sight hadn't been so amazing, Sam would have been anxious to get back to the mural immediately.

A monkey scampered up the rocks to Sam. It stopped and looked up thoughtfully. Sam slowly lowered his camera and let it hang around his neck. Then he pulled out his sketchbook and pencil, moving carefully so he wouldn't scare the monkey.

"Hold that pose, little guy," Sam whispered as his pencil danced across the paper, outlining the shape of the monkey's face. He was concentrating so hard he didn't see Hana and Sofia frantically waving at him from the other side of the steamy pool.

"Sam!" He heard Sofia whisper-shout his name, and he looked up. She was pointing urgently at something to his left, her other finger on her lips. Sam slowly turned his head to look. There, right next to him, was a little monkey holding a brightly painted wooden doll.

Sam gulped and dropped his pencil, which clattered onto the rocks below. Startled, the monkey scrambled across the rocks and out of reach.

"Don't get too close," Hana called softly. "He's probably scared."

Sam steadied himself and tucked his sketch pad into his messenger bag. He caught a glimpse of the apples and had an idea.

The small monkey slipped behind one of the nearby trees. Sam took a few steps and looked through the branches to see if it was still there. The monkey popped back out as if it were playing peekaboo. Sam played along, popping his head around the tree a few times without moving any closer to the macaque. Then he slowly pulled the apple from his bag, placing it on the rock ledge in front of him.

Sam could see Hana and Sofia watching from the other side of the pool, clutching each other nervously. When she saw the apple, Hana gave Sam a smile and a nod. Sofia grinned and gave Sam a big thumbs-up.

Sam was used to waiting for just the right moment to take the perfect photo, and that skill came in handy now. He stood patiently, biting his lip as he waited for the macaque to take the bait.

After a few more moments, the monkey spied the apple and took a step back onto the rocks. Then it cocked its head to one side and studied the piece of fruit carefully. A second later, the monkey dashed forward.

Sam held his breath, waiting to see what the

monkey would do. It opened its other hand, and Sam watched in horror as the doll bounced along the rocks, rolling straight toward the pool of water.

"Nooooo!" Sam cried.

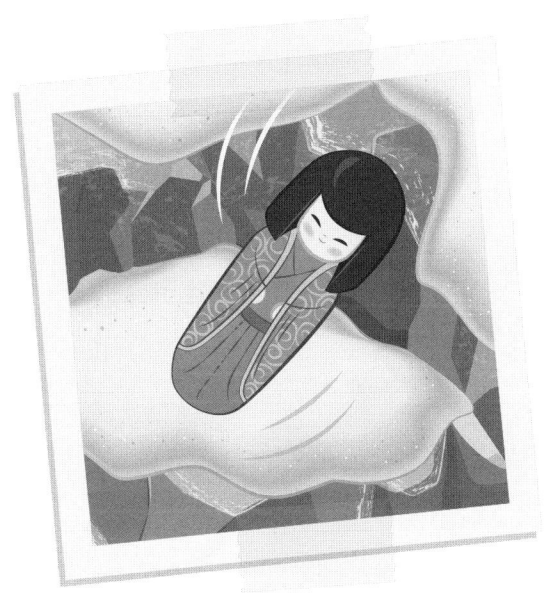

8
Sam's Big Save

Sam leapt forward and whipped his messenger bag off of his shoulder. He threw it out toward the doll, holding onto the strap. The bag landed with a **thwap** on the rocks, and the doll disappeared from view. Sam crept forward. "Please be under the bag, please be under the bag, please be under the bag," Sam muttered to himself. He slowly lifted the bag, gritting his teeth. There was the doll! Sam snatched it up and breathed a huge sigh of relief.

Sofia and Hana dashed around to Sam's side of the pool.

"That was so close!" Sofia said. "Great save, Sam."

"Wow," Hana said.

She took the doll and examined it carefully. It

was a little wet from the snow, but there wasn't a single scratch on it.

"I can't believe we found it," Hana sad. "I was trying to stay hopeful, but I didn't think it was possible. I couldn't have done it without you."

"And we never would have discovered this amazing place without you," Sofia said.

"Thank you for saving my mother's doll, Sam," Hana said.

Sam blushed. "It was no big deal," he said, wiping some pine needles from his vest. "I was just in the right place at the right time. It was like getting the perfect photo. Thank you for leading us to the macaques."

"Speaking of photos..." Sofia motioned toward the macaque, which was perched on a snowy rock at the edge of the pool, happily munching the red apple. The sun was beginning to set behind him, giving the snow a pink-orange glow.

Sam lifted his camera. "Say cheese," he said to the monkey. Then he snapped away.

Click-click!

"I was able to make a few quick sketches, too," Sam said. "I think I have what I need to finish painting the mural now."

Hana glanced at the sun, which was slipping lower and lower behind the trees.

"We better head back down," she said. "Once the sun sets, it's going to get even colder up here."

Sam and Sofia exchanged a glance. The scooter hadn't been charged since that morning. Sam wasn't sure how long the battery would last. Plus, the mural unveiling was that evening! He and Sofia had to get back soon to finish painting the monkey's face.

"Yeah," Sam agreed. "We need to get back, too."

Sofia nodded. "So long, snow monkeys," she called out to the macaques in the trees around them. "It was nice to meet you!"

As if in reply, one of the monkeys scampered right up to the group. It glanced up for a moment, then held something out to them: Sam's pencil!

"Wow," Sam said. "Thanks, little guy." He carefully took his pencil before the monkey dashed back toward the steaming water.

9
Sayonara, Japan!

The way down the snow-covered trail was quicker, but the sun was setting fast, making it difficult for the trio to see the path ahead. Sam slipped in the snow more than once, and his pants were damp and cold.

He, Sofia, and Hana hurried back past Nagano Café and through town to Hana's family's inn.

When Hana slid open the wooden door, they were greeted by the warm, fragrant scent of tea. Hana removed her shoes and placed them near the door, stepping into a pair of slippers.

"We remove our shoes at the door," Hana explained. "It's Japanese tradition. We wear slippers on these wooden floors here. We sit and sleep on the *tatami* floor, where we wear socks or go barefoot."

Sam and Sofia followed their friend's lead and took off their shoes, gratefully stepping into the warm slippers Hana offered them.

A moment later, a woman in a beautiful floral-print kimono appeared.

"Hana-chan," she said. "I thought I heard your voice."

"Hello, Okaasan," Hana said. "These are my friends, Sam and Sofia. This is my mother. She is the *okamisan*. The owner of our inn."

"Welcome," Hana's mother greeted Sam and Sofia with a warm bow. "Please, sit down. I just made some green tea. Can I offer you some?"

"That sounds wonderful," Sofia replied, shivering slightly.

"It looks like you three have been on an adventure," Hana's mother said, her eyes twinkling a bit as she poured their tea.

"You could say that," Hana replied. Then she handed her mother the *kokeshi* doll. "She had a

little adventure, too."

Hana's mother raised an eyebrow at Hana. Sam was worried for a moment that Hana was about to get in trouble, but her mother didn't say a word. She simply took the doll and gently placed it on a shelf full of similar wooden figures.

"She seems happy to be home," Sofia said, admiring the collection. The dolls were all different heights—some tall and some short. Their kimonos were painted different colors and carved or painted with flowers and other intricate designs.

"I think you're right," Hana's mother agreed. Then she smiled. "These dolls remind me of my childhood in Tōhoku. My mother gave me my first one when I was around Hana's age. I've collected them ever since. That's why I named our inn Kokeshi Ryokan."

Sam raised his camera and gestured toward the dolls. "Do you mind?"

Hana's mother smiled and shook her head. "Not at all. And why don't I take one of the three of you?"

Hana, Sam, and Sofia put their arms around each other and grinned at the camera.

"Say cheese," Sam said.

"How do you say 'cheese' in Japanese?" Sofia asked Hana.

"*Chiizu!*" Hana said.

"*Chiizu!*" Sofia repeated.

Click-click!

"It was great meeting you," Sam told Hana. "Your village is a wonderful place."

"You're welcome any time," Hana's mother said. "Next time you can stay at our inn."

"That would be amazing," said Sam. "Thank you for the tea."

"I'll always remember your visit," Hana said. "Thank you again for your help. *Sayonara!*"

Hana waved to them from the doorway as Sam and Sofia hurried down the street toward the parked scooter, which had been blanketed with a layer of fluffy white snow. Sam quickly dusted off the seat and the screen.

"Let's hope this thing is snowproof," Sofia said, tapping the screen. A second later, the glowing globe appeared.

"Phew," Sam breathed a sigh of relief. "I knew Aunt Charlie wouldn't let us down."

He climbed onto the seat and Sofia joined him. The familiar letters asked them where they'd like to travel.

"Time to go home!" Sam said as he typed his reply.

He pressed the green button and the scooter shivered to life. The warm orb of light from the scooter's headlamps and taillights lit up the cold, snowy street. Sam held his breath as the scooter rumbled beneath him.

Whiz . . . Zoom . . . FOOP!

10
Painting Perfection

When Sam opened his eyes, he, Sofia, and the scooter were back in Aunt Charlie's lab.

"That never gets old," Sofia said, climbing off. She dusted her clothes, leaving a little pile of snow on the garage floor.

Sam checked his watch. "We have to hurry," he said. "We don't have much time to finish the mural before the unveiling!"

Sam and Sofia plugged the scooter into the wall, left the garage, and ran to Compass Community Center. A crowd of friends and neighbors had already gathered, and they all stood talking in front of the covered mural.

Sam couldn't believe it. They'd gone all the way to Japan to get what they needed to finish the mural, only to have run out of time.

"We're too late," Sam said.

"Don't be silly," said Sofia.

"They're about to reveal it, and it's not finished!" Sam cried.

Sofia pointed to the bushes next to the mural. "Time for some peekaboo," she said, and Sam smiled.

The pair scurried toward the bushes and hid

behind the leaves. They snuck past the gathering crowd and ducked under the tarp.

Sam knew exactly what he needed to do, but there was one more problem: It was really dark under the tarp! Luckily, Sofia seemed to read his mind.

"Here," she said, leaning forward. She grabbed the camera from around Sam's neck and clicked it on. The camera's small screen gently lit the mural in front of them.

Sam pulled out his sketchbook and looked at what he had drawn as Sofia toggled through the photos on his camera. Sam picked up his brushes and got right to work.

The soft glow of the camera's screen reminded him of the sun glistening through the steam

of the monkey's hot spring. It was the perfect inspiration as he quickly painted the details of the macaque's face.

Finally, he sat back and looked up, smiling.

"It looks just like the monkey from the rocks," Sofia said, smiling.

"He's just missing the apple," Sam said.

Sofia reached into the messenger bag and

pulled out the last of Mr. Ogawa's apples.

"Here you go," she said, and the two laughed.

Sam and Sofia slipped out from under the tarp and joined the small crowd that had gathered for the unveiling. They found Aunt Charlie right away.

"There you two are! You ready?" Aunt Charlie asked. She stood next to Lyla and Luiz, Sofia's mother and father, who both beamed with pride. Mama Lyla was the director of Compass Community Center, where Papai Luiz ran the art program. They'd been the ones to encourage Sam and Sofia to paint the mural in the first place.

"It took a lot of work," Sam said, "but it's finally done."

Mama Lyla turned to the crowd. "And are you all ready?" she called out.

Everyone clapped and cheered in response.

Sam held his breath as he waited for the tarp

to be removed.

"Let us present to you," Lyla said, "Animals Around the World!"

Together, Lyla, Sam, Sofia, and Aunt Charlie pulled down the tarp to reveal the painting. The crowd gasped with delight and broke into applause.

Sam smiled. The macaque's face looked even better in the full light.

Aunt Charlie put her arm around his shoulder. "You should be proud of yourself, Sam," she said. "The animals all look so realistic. And that macaque's face is impressive! I bet you couldn't have done better if you'd actually gone to Japan to find a real live monkey."

Sam and Sofia exchanged a look as Aunt Charlie gave them a wink.

11
Home Again

Once Sam was home, he headed straight to his bedroom to put away his art supplies. He placed the jar of Aunt Charlie's rust-colored paint on the shelf next to his desk, which was crowded with other paints, markers,

and brushes. Sam's easel stood across the room, where he'd drawn his original sketch of the mural. He smiled as he thought of the finished painting on the wall of the community center.

Then he sprawled out on his bed and began flipping through the photos on his camera. He paused when he came to the image of himself, Sofia, and Hana at the Kokeshi Ryokan, with the shelf of dolls behind them. This would be the perfect addition to the wall of photos on display above his desk. He would hang it right next to the picture of himself, Sofia, and Lucas in the Amazon rainforest in Brazil.

Suddenly, Sam remembered something. He reached into his pocket and carefully pulled out the intricately folded origami macaque. Just looking at the tiny creation made him think of his new friend Hana, cooking *onsen-tamago*, and his amazing photo shoot with the monkeys near the snowy mountain hot spring. Sam knew he would never forget his amazing adventure with Sofia in Japan.

The paper had been flattened in his pocket, but the origami animal was still intact. He carefully smoothed the folds and placed the little monkey on the shelf with his art supplies.

"There," he said aloud. "Welcome to Compass Court, little guy."

Ping!

Sam's computer chimed. He had an incoming video call. He went over to his desk and accepted it. A moment later, Sofia's grinning face filled his screen.

"Hey, Sam!" she said.

"Hi Sofia," he replied. "I'm glad you called. You can say hi to an old friend."

He moved the computer so Sofia could see the little origami snow monkey perched on his shelf.

"Hey little buddy," Sofia said, waving. "He fits right in."

"What's up?" Sam asked.

"Well, my mom just told me that there's going to be a gigantic yard sale in a few weeks to raise money for Compass Community Center," she said, her voice full of excitement.

"That's cool," Sam said.

"Cool?!" Sofia replied. "Sam, this is the best news ever. My mom said we have permission to

go into the attic to search for stuff to sell. I know there are some amazing old treasures up there."

Sofia's eyes sparkled. Sam just grinned. He had a feeling he and Sofia would be off on another adventure in no time at all.

おしまい

Oshimai
(The End)

Japanese Terms

- chan - A term of endearment added to the end of a name

- Chiizu - Cheese

- Geta - Wooden shoes

- Kokeshi - Japanese wooden dolls, originated in Tohoku

- Saru - Monkey

- Okaasan - Mother

- Okamisan - Inn owner

- Onsen - Hot spring

- Onsen-tamago - Egg dish soft-boiled in an onsen

- Ryokan - Traditional Japanese inn

- Tatami - Traditional mats made of straw

- Yukata - Lightweight cotton kimono, worn at hot springs

Japanese Phrases

- Arigatō gozaimasu - Thank you

- Gochisosama - Thank you for the meal

- Gomen nasai - I'm sorry

- Hai - Yes

- Itadakimasu - Let's eat / I'm receiving this meal

- Sayonara - Goodbye

Portuguese Words

- Papai - Dad

- Vamos! - Let's go!

Sofia and Sam's Snippets

Japan is made up of four main islands and thousands of smaller islands. The four main islands are called Hokkaido, Honshu, Shikoku, and Kyushu.

Hokkaido

Honshu

Tokyo

Capital of Japan

Shikoku

Kyushu

Thousands of years ago, some Japanese islands were connected to Siberia and Korea by land bridges, allowing people to walk across. A string of islands, like Japan, is called an archipelago.

The Japanese concept of **wa**, which means harmony, focuses on the greater good of the community rather than personal needs. The Japanese people value hard work and respect.

Nagano Prefecture is an area of Japan surrounded by three mountain ranges, all part of the Japanese Alps: Hida, Kiso, and Akaishi.

The land nestled at the base of these mountains is perfect for growing apples. Farmers have become known for the Nagano apple, a local specialty.

Nagano apple

Two Japanese islands, Tashirojima and Aoshima, are home to more cats than humans. On Tashirojima especially, cats are believed to be good luck.

Origami is one of many Japanese art forms. **Ikebana** (floral art), **shodō** (calligraphy), **kabuki** (stage drama), **buyō** (traditional dance), and more are practiced in Japan.

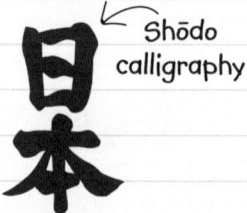

← Shōdo calligraphy

"Japan" (written as "nihon" in Japanese)

There are more than 10,000 trees growing in Tokyo's Shinjuku Gyoen National Garden. It includes an English garden, a formal French garden, and traditional Japanese gardens.

It's famous for its cherry blossoms, which bloom every year in March and April.

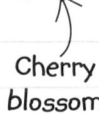
Cherry blossom

Onsen-tamago is one of many delicious Japanese dishes. Fish, rice, and vegetables are staples in Japanese cooking, which is known for its fresh flavors and healthy ingredients.

Japan leads the world in the field of robotics. Japanese engineers have created a variety of different robots, including some that look and move like people.

How to Make an Origami Monkey

Instructions:

1. Fold and unfold a square piece of paper down the middle to create a crease.

2. Fold each side corner inward to meet in the middle at the crease.

3. Fold the bottom point backward.

4. Fold in half.

5. Turn to the right.

6. Bend the point downward, lifting the sides to open the "pocket."

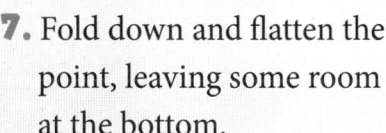

7. Fold down and flatten the point, leaving some room at the bottom.

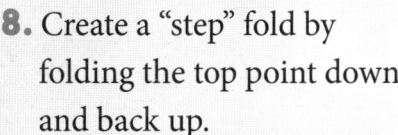

8. Create a "step" fold by folding the top point down and back up.

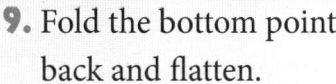

9. Fold the bottom point back and flatten.

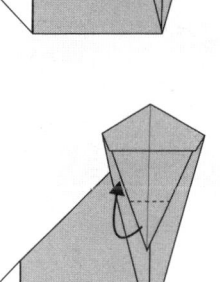

10. Draw the monkey's face!

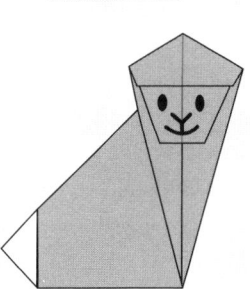

Keep your adventure going with a Science Expeditions subscription!

Solve real-world mysteries with fun, hands-on activities.

Ages 9+

Fun activities come to life with exciting, action-packed experiments. Launch your very own catapult, propel an air-powered rocket, and create ooey-gooey slime!

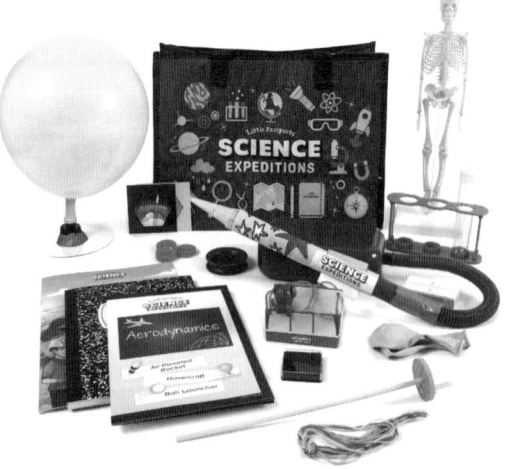

LittlePassports.com/Science